The Twenty-Five Fifties

The Twenty-Five Fifties

Shane Bunnag

RIVER BOOKS

First published in Thailand in 2025 by
River Books Press Co., Ltd
396/1 Maharaj Road, Phraborommaharajawang,
Bangkok 10200 Thailand
Tel: (66) 2 225-0139, 2 225-9574
Email: order@riverbooksbk.com
www.riverbooksbk.com
@riverbooks riverbooksbk Riverbooksbk

Publisher: River Books Press Ltd., Bangkok, Thailand
EU Authorised Representative: Easy Access System Europe Oü, 16879218 - Mustamäe tee 50, 10621 Tallinn, Estonia, gpsr.requests@easproject.com

Publisher: Narisa Chakrabongse
Design: Shane Bunnag & Ruetairat Nanta

ISBN 978 616 451 108 8

The cover design uses a detail from a temple mural at Wat Khao Krailart, Hua Hin.

Printed and bound in Thailand by Parbpim Co., Ltd

For my dad: traveller, storyteller.

For my family.

THE HILLS

Our hero, the Boy, under the influence of a spirit, steals a motorbike, and takes to the road where he is harangued by a tramp, and given insights into the nature of time from a grilled chicken vendor and some emaciated cows, after which the Boy loses the bike, and joins a work-team cutting a road through the mountainside.

The bike had a pearl-green finish and was fully customised. Its owner had spent a lot of time on the details. The boy liked the bike from the moment he set eyes on it. Of all the bikes there at the meet, this was the one.

The boy was seventeen years old, skinny, clad in denim, body tipped with frizzled-up hair and canvas shoes. As the dancing grew wilder than joy, it turned to flailing with fists and feet. The participants trembled with excitement and forgot themselves and the boy waited, soon a keychain was just within reach.

Who wouldn't have taken it? Reasoned the voice in the boy's head. He didn't reckon on the voice being more than his own.

The spirit had been unaware of the comings and goings of the multitude until the music began. The pulsating noise reached into the night wilds, a persistent entity of hysterical proportions: bass and treble and vocals, all turning to limbs and heads. The sound brought back passions. After its long rest on the forest floor, the spirit suddenly wanted to know life, and was transported to the music.

Beyond the hilly woodland was flat terrain, covered in orchards and shacks. By a host of dragon-fruit, a thousand or so youngsters had gathered for a concert. They came and went on motorbikes. The road leading to the field busy with vehicles and vendors, with shouts and cheers.

The spirit looked down at the festival and remembered war, and was stirred. It alighted on the tendril of a fruiting plant at the edge of the campsite, close to the boy.

But the boy, overtaken by desire for the bike, was untouched by the presence of the equanimous spirit. His bike love pulled the spirit to his ear, to murmur: let's go, come on, let's go and see what's out there.

Leaving the others to the uncritical stamping, the boy took off on the pearl-green motorbike. When they noticed his absence, they said: he's gone home, got bored. It'll take him days, over the mountain and across the river. We'll beat him with an iron bar when we find him, stab and dump him in a canal.

The boy tore through the night hills. At first, he raced beside others but passing a petrol station and a sleeping town he was alone.

The boy was very high, happy in not thinking, and not dreaming. In his wakeful oblivion the boy cheered to himself, not questioning why he was on the bike and where he might be going. It felt good, he'd have stroked the bike's gorgeous fenders – beautiful, humming machine – if he hadn't been gripping the handlebar.

He remained in this blurred hypnosis as the dawn broke: red breaking through the dark for a moment before the day came in grey and brittle.

When the spirit was a man, he had made music, and loved, and lived in a village full of barking dogs. In the year of the Boar, during the waxing moon in the eleventh month, he had been marched off to fight, in a vast and ravenous troop. They had rolled across the land shrieking.

His human life ended by the edge of a marsh, where he was found by a hunter who put him in a piece of stone which was slung in a pouch around the hunter's waist. When at last the hunter died in the forest, the stone spirit remained by the trunk of a large tree.

Mid-morning the boy arrived in a small town. Sobering, he needed something to pep himself back up. He went to the convenience store, a little orderly world – three rows of products, a wall of refrigerated drinks, bright over-head lights even during the day, everything in its place. Nothing of any great use, price or good. It was the continuation of the mind that planned the provincial town and the streets and lights that radiated outwards and across the country connecting to each other like a sacred map, those arteries of a nation turned into cheap wiring. A man was waiting for a grilled sandwich at the counter, while feral-looking children dashed in front of bored girls at the till. Exiting the shop, with water and worker's drink, the boy was blocked by a tramp, who lowered himself to the ground and grovelled.

Spirit, he said. Please accept my offering. Then he held out a crisp and improbable bank note for the boy to take.

The tramp remembered, for the benefit of the spirit, how they all came from the valleys between the steep hills, where they were due to return someday, to the narrow space between water and vapour. Did he recall, the tramp went on, how they used to raid the lowlands? The coming and going had exhausted their adversaries. A destiny formed in fighting, would revert soon to primordial steam.

Boy, the tramp preached. You think it is a matter of one foot following the other. Steps rising through this country to pass the cities to your home but there is no map to show how to navigate the place in your heart, from being a boy to becoming someone who knows and sees. Because if you knew and saw, you'd have a different approach. You might have started out elsewhere. However, since you are taking your steps and are set upon a path, go forward with your eyes open and we shall meet again.

The syrupy drink gave the boy a kick, but soon his eyes were tired and began to falter under the baking sun. He skidded to a brief stop by the roadside and drained his water. Two skinny cows stared from a dry allotment. They nodded at him, the only person they had seen in an eternity. Don't stop here, they told him. Here is madness and death. You'll end with bones like ours that melt under the sun, glued to the spot as the world speeds past, a world that can never stop or see us, and that cannot save us.

The boy drove the bike away from this further emptiness, this piece of sleepless hell and scanned for a suitable place to rest.

Spotting a bus shelter, he pulled himself onto the platform and took off his jacket, to use as a cover, and passed out, leaving the scene as a teenager can, with the shelter spinning around him.

The spirit watched from a branch nearby, before coming down and perching again inside the boy's ear.

The boy woke up four times. The first time he was surrounded by school children, the second time by factory workers returning from their shift, the third time by the passage of a ritual procession. When the boy woke for the fourth time his bike was gone.

He was sad. But hunger overtook his grief, so he bought grilled pork from a vendor, while he asked about his bike. You won't have seen another like it. Truly.

We are made of the same stuff. The vendor cackled. She was going to the next town and offered him a lift on her grill wagon.

In our speed we experience the same seconds as those on the side of the road. The vendor called over the wagon putter.

Filled with every tree, the goat that walks in that patch, all these cars and trucks, the changing light, the buildings as we pass – we experience all these many details in the time they see just the dust beneath their feet. We live more, and longer and time slows. In plying this road for a year, I live ten normal years. With my two decades of travel, I am ancient to the bone.

She left the boy at a crossroads where he caught a lift with a truck driver.

The cabin was musty from air-conditioning. The music on the radio was melodic and mournful; a song of struggle, a soundtrack for a life on the roads. The boy drifted off, into the words of the song, gritty poetry from a mouth that has tasted bitterness; yet outside the trees fanned up to the sky. The trucks ahead were brushed by leaf, the snake-scale road enveloped in green, brown and yellow, patterned and delicate as lace.

Coming out of his reverie, the boy saw a line of cars ahead. The truck stationary in a deep-set road, hemmed by verdant nature.

Wake up, get out. The police have blocked traffic. I can't have you here. The trucker growled. You're on your own.

The boy climbed down and walked by the vehicles towards the checkpoint. The police ignored him as he stepped around the tented post, continuing with their tasks. He soon came to a group sitting in the shade at the roadside. They stared at him as he approached. As he reached them, the nearest asked where he was going. The boy told them how he lost his bike and asked if they had seen it. A sympathetic figure explained their ride was on its way through the checkpoint, he could come if he wanted.

There were four of them, one was asleep. The others welcomed the boy to sit on the ground, share their drink. A woman muttered at the spirit on the boy's shoulder, I see you, what mischief are you up to? Causing the spirit to flitter back into the boy's ear.

They finished the bottle in the back of the van, where a couple of hammocks had been strung up, suspended above loose cargo that was lashed down, as to a ship's deck. The boy was billeted in the vessel, a rolling piece of spiritual lumber full of hot liquor.

After a time, one of the men turned to the boy and said: Look we're going this way, why don't you come and work with us for a few days. It's easy and they're always in need of hands. Make a bit of money and then you can catch a bus home.

At the end of the dirt road, above a long climb, the men stepped down and looked into the valley. The jungle fell off into a waste of red earth, where gangs of men worked machines building a wide road against the land, each one covered from head to foot in rags, sock-like arm pulls, home-made balaclavas denying the brightness, ragged scarves and over-sized boots.

A foreman, standing on powdered rocks above a world of ramparts and ditches, took in the boy. He'll work, they said. Then they took him to eat. In a makeshift village, of scraps of board and corrugated iron, and fresh branches from the old forest, they crouched around a pot and served up some rice and soup and fried meat.

That afternoon they worked, and in the night the boy slept in a hovel with the rest of the men.

He did this for a time without asking much. When the foreman gave the boy some money, he paid back the others for his food and board.

Would you stay on? They asked him. The boy told them he should leave and see if he could find his bike. Don't worry, if you stay and work with us you can buy another just like it.

Impossible, he told them.

The locals didn't like the road. They were against it and for some reason, from the day the works started, everything went wrong. The bosses couldn't hold on to their workers. For months, machines were sabotaged in the night, the work was plagued by accidents. Extra hands were brought in from far away.

Eventually the big men sent in some guns. The killers would come through the camp twitching with adrenalin, like they'd been on a hunt. Over time things were quieter and the problems ended soon enough. Now everyone was happy. You could see smiles wherever you looked.

When the boy slept, the spirit climbed out of his ear. It explored, but never far from the camp. There was much to take in, so it convinced the boy to stay on a little longer and keep working. The road was a curious prospect. The spirit wanted to see how these things came about, the highways that changed everything.

THE WOODS

The Boy is abandoned to a gang of feral children, who are fascinated by his companion spirit. Locked into a bamboo cage by the children, the Boy is taunted by the sound of his beloved motorbike.

One morning his friends called him to their truck, asking if he'd like to make some extra cash, since they had the day off.

The truck bumped along a dirt road for an hour passing a signpost, this a concrete rendering of a sawn-through log below a string of weathered letters.

At the old guardhouse, the boy was sent down to shift a rusting metal barrier. They then made their way up and then down into a welcoming area overwhelmed by leaves and fallen trees. The shops and ticket office had crumbled; the forest had merged with the man-made. The van travelled on, crashing through and whipping past groves of thick bamboo and green that tumbled over the road. The men called out, shouting into the drunken landscape.

As they forded a stream, a cloud of butterflies, as black as a girl's hair, rose up. The old resort was further along the river, by the rapids. Its wooden cabins were set about a curve in the riverbank, each with a porch: suburban utopias in the heart of chaos. The forlorn space was dotted with wild animals: a grinning bear clapping its paws together, monkeys riding a tiger's back, misshapen elephants and grazing deer, the latter blissfully unaware of the predators that prowled beside them.

The men joked as they unloaded their tools, then set about stripping down metal, from old air conditioners, wiring, plumbing, wrenching strips from the junk furniture and hideous public sculpture.

The boy was given a hammer and some pliers but wandered around the lost campsite before sitting down on a cement bench to look at the passing water. He heard the others calling to each other, and then their shouts.

With the hubbub, he ran back past the bungalows, just in time to see the truck disappearing down the road leaving a train of dust, and a bag of tools spilled over the ground.

Reaching down for the bag, the boy felt eyes on him.

Standing twenty metres away were children covered in grime, with matted hair. The three he saw were joined by more, who stepped out of the thicket in silence.

The boy stood rooted to the ground hopelessly as the children surrounded him.

The summer camp children never left. Their families had never collected them. The children learned to live in the trees. They hunted, built traps. They smeared themselves in mud like elephants against the sun and the insects, and devised their own faith and cosmology.

The park of broken sculptures, those forest animals: bears, deer, elephants, tigers, serpents – all rendered in concrete and daubed with thin paint – were now elaborated into comforting idols by the savage children.

The boy was led gently by his hosts into their world, recalled to his past life. The deaths of his parents, the government orphanage and the times he ran.

The children spoke their own language, one that the boy had never heard before. They gestured to him and refused to answer in his tongue even though they seemed to understand what he was saying. But they were kind to him.

The children took him to their house, formerly the park information centre, where they slept on the floor. They showed him how they fished in the river, and cooked their catch wrapped up in leaves.

The boy drew pictures of his motorbike in the dirt. They jabbed at the image in excitement, and he showed them how it was to ride such a beauty, until he grew disconsolate.

The Woods

The spirit knew that they could see him. It pleased him, he asked them questions about where they had come from and how long they had been there. Alongside the motorbike, the children drew symbols that the boy couldn't read but the spirit accepted.

They made fragile offerings out of the jungle and left them at the foot of the boy's bed.

After a car intruded, the children led the boy out of the visitors' centre into the woods and put him in a cage made from bamboo. It was well wrought. The boy wondered how long it took them to make it.

He heard his old friends calling his name and listened impotently as the car left again. The children didn't come back to the cage that night. He slept uneasily.

When he woke up the next morning there was a bottle of water by the cage door and some fruit. Seeing the votive motorbike threaded from grass, he knew the children wouldn't come back.

The forest seemed louder, hotter.

He pushed at the cage door and pulled at the woven walls and shouted. The spirit saw that the boy was upset and decided that now was the time. It spoke to the boy: I'll be here with you, right here inside your ear. The boy replied, I don't want your guidance, all I wanted was freedom.

Can I go with the children who want me?

Only if you give me something, said the boy.

What would that be?

Something incandescent, then I'll be able to sleep again.

The boy liked his gift but felt lonely after the spirit was gone. He lay fitfully in his cell, imagining what would happen to him.

With the dawn came a sound. The boy shot up and grasped the bamboo bars, ten times the tensile strength of steel. But no match for him as the sound drew closer. The hum of the pearl-green bike was unmistakable. Who had come to taunt him? The bike circled the cage, out of sight, chuckling into the break of day. He screamed and stamped, promising vengeance. The bike came close and stopped. The boy registered footsteps, and the sound of urination. He shook the cage, and found the spot where the children's hands had missed a loop of twine.

By the time the boy had slid out of the trap the bike was gone. He wept at the track-marks and cursed the trickster who had stolen his ride. Powerless, the boy followed a trail into the woods. He cried at the thought of the machine getting muddy, its chain rusting, those peerless spokes caught by wayside twigs and swamp vine.

THE JUNGLE

The Boy strays into the forest, meeting a lady who dreams of grafting an orchid onto her body.

Noticing a flower hanging from a branch, the boy reached unthinking to place it behind an ear. He really had no time for such matters, but it was this senseless action that undid all the good work. Had it not been months since the boy had had a sign from the bike? Now that he was close, tempted and teased by the other thief, he had found a flower, and lost the trail.

Bewildered by the lack of good fortune, the boy ambled into a clearing, and there on a long banqueting table, covered in a white cloth, was a feast. He stepped past delicacies, curries, two kinds of rice, snacks steamed and fried, sauces and condiments. He was about to steal a parcel of chicken cooked in pandan leaf, when a man in a white suit banged him over the head with a wooden spoon. For this injustice, the boy launched himself at the waiter, to fall into empty space. The servant was quick.

The boy was outnumbered. He felt his arms pulled back, knees bent to the floor. Two more of the white suits had appeared out of nowhere, they held him down and said they would let him go as soon as he promised not to make a scene. There must be order when the ladies returned, they warned. The boy had no option but to nod, and choke out: Have you seen a bike by any chance?

The waiters had not noticed. They told him that they had been busy with the picnic. It was no small feat to carry the tables and chairs, the hampers, drinks, and food, all this way, up from the nearest track, with no path, and wild animals at every turn. But the pay was good.

They would have told him more about their work, and the boy suspected they were about to offer him a job when a party of girls stepped out of the trees and crossed the clearing. The women were dressed in khaki uniforms, with trousers tucked into socks against leeches. They struggled along with nets and shears and pincer tipped sticks, and a lightweight ladder. One held a parasol above a lady, with a dignified air, who walked directly to the boy, smiling, and plucking from his head the flower.

Come now, tell me where you found that one. What a specimen. The grand old lady said, now seated. The boy kept his wits, and replied that he'd help her as soon as she told him where he could find his motorbike. But the grand lady was not having it. She rolled her eyes and said that he could talk to her son about bikes, and inquired among the waiters and her female attendants, who told her that the young man had not been seen all day.

The girls brought the boy slices of tart, quiche, cupcakes, and puddings, they piled on ice cream and coconut dessert, and gave him pink fizzy drinks, and green soda pop. He ate and spluttered, while the lady pored through a book on flowers and said. Remarkable.

There was no choice. The boy suspected that her son had taken his bike. Perhaps, he reasoned, if he waited just a little longer, the thief would appear. He led the party back across the clearing, into the forest. The boy felt he should be an expert for the sake of the company, but he had no names, or stories to give. He was not even sure if this had been the way he had come.

The lady spoke about orchids, and picked several along the way, pointing out their features, and delights. Her attendants, the young women, giggled, telling the boy that she was out looking for flowers to put her name to. That was why the lady had to have a rare orchid from the deep jungle. Every year, in the season, she arranged a hunting trip, and every year she went home empty-handed.

That evening, after berating the boy, for being brown and filthy, she sulked in her tent. The waiters said that she had been weeping, looking at the perfect specimen wilting by her book on botany.

They travelled further into the woods. The boy pitied his companions, and gave a hand, rushing back and forth with a bottle of gas, tent pegs, trunks full of cutlery and tablecloths, ferrying the necessaries from nameless place to place.

It was when the butter ran out that the search was called off. She was beside herself, and gave the boy a hug, commiserating about his bike and her plight. The lady claimed to be without merit, she gave so much but the forest never cared. He wanted to know why she did it, and the lady undid her shirt. The boy averted his eyes for a moment, then she touched him, and he looked past her sweaty beige bra at a wound on her inner arm.

Don't listen to those girls, their heads are full of air. It's not for vanity that I search, I have a grander scheme. My greatest desire is to graft a flower to my skin. But it must be the right bloom.

She showed him her sketches. The boy admired her draughtsmanship, the seamlessness of the lady burning up in bright orchid colours. Florid wings lifting the woman above society, out of reach of mushroom hair, and porcelain skin, and wrinkle-free faces.

As consolation, the boy showed her the gift from the spirit, and watching him she dabbed her eyes, and said, how was it that one so lowly and stupid had been granted both the rare flower and the ineffable gift? He replied that he wanted neither, if only he could get his bike back, but she was not listening, she looked away dreamily, saying that she would be back again next year.

THE HERMIT

A hermit takes the Boy under his wing, and tells him stories of Siamese Armageddon.

Like you I was from a city. I lived in the capital, was born, schooled, and worked there. I even had a family for a time. I couldn't stay. It consumed me. Do you recall those days sitting in traffic? The exhaust fumes belching out, sunlight streaming down on an endless sea of cars. The days before the city was covered up with flyovers. I was devoured by the city. It came to me suddenly, the terror. Without announcing itself, the fear arrived and took shape.

The dubious holy-man was talking rapidly, mumbling through his story. The boy, sitting on the ground on a large leaf, looked up at the older man, perched on a rock.

I left my wife, I abandoned my children. I never looked back to see my parents. I had to leave, and that also came to me suddenly. But we are not alike. You who never had a family, or anyone who cared.

I had a bike, the boy wanted to tell him, but he knew the time was not right.

Somehow, the hermit found the boy wandering in the forest, left by the orchid hunters to his own fate.

The man was middle-aged, not dressed in a white robe, just wild looking, insane from spending so much time alone. He found the boy and led him to his camp. He had been living in these woods for a long time; untethered from society and norms. He told of how he was once an ordinary city person, with a nice family and job and then one day he gradually lost the thread of his existence. When he finally left, it was simple enough – perhaps a strange blessing to those closest to him.

Over days in the forest the hermit told his story. The boy helped him to collect jungle greens and herbs that he traded with the villagers for rice and fish-sauce. The locals came to him for advice and fortune-telling, they treated him like a holy-man but he made no claims.

He knew about the nature of destruction. The deaths of a nation that come in saltwater waves, and in blackened and poisonous fresh water, in sinkings, drownings, fire – in the country fields, in the mind and the city streets. Ends brought by homemade explosives, bullets, bombings, lynchings, car-wrecks. Destruction wrought by economic collapse and the falling apart of reason and belief. The puncturing of illusions and the crumbling of idols. Angst driven by false seers and made flesh by leaders. Damnation precipitated by liars and hypocrites. Inertia spread by hypnosis, celebrity magazines and grand society events. Sleepwalkers following the blind, and the myopic chasing a tune blaring from a deserted shopping mall. Terminal days, and fading punctuations depicted on temple walls, daubed around the insides of caves and scrawled upon abandoned buildings off crowded streets – stinking of shit and rot. Warnings that came from the earliest times, only to be forgotten and ignored by each passing generation. So many silenced prognosticators, with their countless stories all laughed into wordlessness. Forced grins and nullified body language, the articulation of rage through immobility.

These were some of the ways an end is heralded, louder and louder through the urban calendar and yet muted by laughter and polished smiles.

If you see so much, can you tell me how to find my beloved motor scooter? The boy asked, almost at a whisper. But the hermit was also hard of hearing.

My words are filled with sand that drags them out of shape.

The hermit tried to tell those around him, to point out the resonances, the evidence, but he soon realised it was both impossible and dangerous.

He could not go on.

I can't go on. He had shouted.

One day he got out of bed and pulled on some clothes. He walked out of the house, into the night, without looking back. He kept going until he was out of town. He lived rough along the national highways and over time ended up in the forest. After the fighting was over, he wanted to find peace. People came to him, with offerings, food. He started leaving them things he found along his way: curious rocks, carved baubles, herbs, fruit. He realised that even if people were not willing to give up their lives, that deep down they recognised the true nature of things, this was their way of honouring it by placing one such as him on a small pedestal.

It could not go on. The hermit continued. This disconnection between daily existence and the true nature of things. The idolatry could not go on. There had to be a break, where one side gives in. When the one side surrenders, we will be given a chance to rebuild. Let the flood come for us. Let the teaming city burst its banks and rush into the wilds to be broken up and absorbed. Let the fear of the forest burst out across the highways and down the rivers and go swelling into the urban spaces, sending the buildings running in mad terror. Let the two sides experience the panic.

I am just another bit of debris carried along on these waters that sweep through the country, said the hermit.

We live in a time of strife. These troubles will not leave much standing and by the time they have passed there may be very little left of what we once held dear. The land itself may have changed, been taken by the water, the cities rendered uninhabitable. If we knew of what is to come wouldn't all those who have been fighting cease and take common cause? No, blindness is upon us and the voices of caution and reason are inaudible in this shouting match.

In such days, where we speak of two warring sides, everything seems political. It appears from the outside as if everyone has already chosen a camp, and from the inside we are too torn to see how our choices and beliefs are determined by emotive factors. I reject that people are political in their choices. Most are swept along by events and do their best to stay close to the people they care for. The whole mass is gathered up by a few wills, those few who know how to shout and feel the thrill of leadership. But what sorry leaders we see.

Boy, tell me what is it that you desire to know? These forests here are the beginning and end of what we call this country. All that you might search for is ready to be witnessed, experienced. All lessons are on offer. You have only to observe fully, learn by heart, then break apart; it's simple, you'll see. Now, walk with me through the woods. Let us explore the higher ground.

THE OUTPOST

The Boy and his current patron, the fake holy man, climb to an old insurgent base, which has become a tourist viewpoint, and the Boy is finally sent on his way.

They passed through an afternoon, stopping to catch their breath along a track and to drink water at a stream. The sun beat down upon them as they stepped out into an opening in the bush. The boy felt dizzy under the light after so long in the forest. It was as if he'd stepped from a cave into the middle of a glaring desert. They made their way through a sea of waist-high grass, razor-like, that clung to their clothes and grazed their limbs as they moved. On the other side of the meadow they pushed through bamboo, as dense as a prop wall in some tele-drama. They untangled onto a stony plateau. The hermit led the way in silence. As they crossed this rocky terrain, he began to talk about the days he'd spent up there fighting the government soldiers. He touched craters and cracks in the surface. He glanced at forgotten bullet holes like old friends. Still hidden by bushes was an old artillery piece, anchored into the stone and rusted useless, a piece of historic junk.

My job when I first came here was to bring ordnance down from the main camp to supply the gunners. First, we'd get the stuff through the jungles. It had been smuggled across the river, then overland by car and truck in small quantities and then finally up these hills on carts and the back of beast and man. Then we'd have it stored up in the caves, protected from the elements and from government bombing raids. We had so much to do each day that there was never a moment to wonder if any of us had made the right decision. I carried shells down here, up there and all around for months before they taught me to operate the guns. I had a knack for operating the mortar. It's mainly a question of geometry. Not that we were too serious. This was just for show, keeping the government troops in the lowlands – nothing too specific or targeted.

The hermit hastened the boy onwards, leaving the rusted cannon alone to the elements. He continued. It took me a few months to get here. I stole up through the towns and the provincial cities, we had sympathisers, and they helped. I kept moving until I reached the wilds, barely touched by roads, much larger and still sprawling. There were many villages in the forests in those days, and no real law and order, no real government – there never had been. They were suspicious when I first arrived. I was locked up for a few days for interrogation and then released and kept at another lower camp. They did their background checks, they observed. I bumped into an old friend from the university by chance and he vouched for me. He'd been underground for a year already. I had no idea, thought he'd dropped out.

The boy and the hermit were slipping uphill, the way was slick with mud and water dripping down the mossy rocks. The hermit was pointing into the caves and checkpoints of the life he led up in these mountains.

So, you came here to fight? The boy asked.

I came here to live, said the holy-man. The fighting was a necessity. I wasn't doctrinaire.

If you wanted to live, couldn't you have just hidden in the city and been forgotten? asked the boy.

My friends were all on the run. Many were dead. My family was under watch. I came here and soon I started to believe. The fighting made me believe. We thought we could build a better world. We thought everything would change.

Their way through the wilderness ended abruptly. There was a clean and freshly painted flight of wooden steps leading down from the old communist camp. They walked down and through the overhanging rocks, each cave there well marked with accompanying text on placards along the way. If the boy had taken the time to stop and pay attention to all of these writings he'd have seen the rebel hospital area, the shelter used during bombing raids. He would have seen the jail cells, and the dormitory area. They passed through and out of the forest onto tarmac. A few more metres around the next corner and they were walking past a restaurant with a picture menu displayed in front and a pretty floral arrangement spilling from pill boxes along its terrace. The owner, a middle-aged woman with large hair, looked up from her counter and beamed to the hermit. She stood at the entrance of the diner and raised her hands in prayer.

Hello, she said and laughed. We haven't seen you for a while. How are you keeping?

Like the trees and like the rocks. I go on. I change but there is no one there to notice.

Can I offer you anything, a drink, food?

The hermit shook his head and smiled. The boy followed him past the old lady. I see you have found a disciple. She laughed, throwing the words over her shoulder as she climbed back towards her counter. He's just a stray dog. Arrived looking for food, will disappear when he's had his fill or scents a bitch. The hermit shouted back and continued.

That lady. She was up here in the old days. Good fighter. A real believer right through the years. She even stayed here after the amnesty. Could have gone back to the city but she stayed on, her heart full of melancholy about the fight. Head full of regret about the world she prayed for. We never thought it was just another utopian mirage. A stop on the way to our final end.

The road gave onto a larger street lined by pines, and clapboard houses, with immaculate lawns, leading to a cluster of larger concrete buildings under a pristine flag.

This was our central command post. The HQ of revolution in this province. Now it is a museum. Inside are some mouldy books, a few guns and trophies, faded photographs, the worn clothing found in these deserted woods, there's not much from those days to honour our dead, our hopes and dreams and disasters.

Every year there are two gatherings up here. Both arrive in tour buses, the same company of cartoon painted coaches. The men are the same age. One lot fought for the government, they come up here to celebrate victory and get drunk in their enemy's haunts. The other group, my lot, lived here and bled here. They come and get drunk and belligerent in the same way and sing the old songs and tell the stories and cry about how they gave in and went soft and live good lives down in the plain.

One year the two groups came on the same day. They had their meal in that restaurant we just passed; took over the whole place and set up long banqueting tables. The veterans were nice to each other. Some of them had become friends and family and work acquaintances. They started drinking and singing and making merry.

Then they started fighting. A whole museum load of relics beating each other up over a forgotten war. The police arrived and told them off. The old folk left on reasonable terms. They calmed down and shared a few more drinks and the police joined in and then everyone was forced to stand by the flagpole and sing the national anthem. That was our revolution.

They were standing by that same flagpole. The hermit reached into his shoulder bag and held out a wallet to the boy.

Here take this.

I don't need it.

There's some money inside. Enough to see you on your way.

But what if I'm not ready to go? said the boy.

Do you still dream about that bike?

I think I'm over it now.

Good, you're done then.

But I'm happy here.

You'll be back here before long, don't worry. Walk down the road. In a few kilometres you'll see a village, and along the route you'll find what you're looking for. Go home if you can.

LOWLANDS

Falling into the company of foreign pilgrims, the Boy is taken to a UFO landing site, he steals a bicycle and has an erotic moment with a bored receptionist, who turns him into a dog. The dog-boy ends up at a temple, where a kind monk saves him from being bitten by a pack of mutts.

The boy's rhythm picked up on the downhill, swirling down the way. A seedpod scattering out of the trees onto the road and through the nascent farmlands. Fields of tapioca gave way to scrublands, and these to an arid plain. The boy staggered under the sun, wondering why he had allowed the hermit to chase him off. He wished he had stayed in the uplands, where his clothes were always damp. He pulled up his jacket to shade his head and staggered onwards.

A bus beeped him out of the road, and then wheezed to a stop beside him. The driver yelled through the open door that he could die out there. The boy kept walking but the bus driver went apace with him, asking questions, did he come from those parts, what was his favourite football team, did he have a girlfriend? The boy asked the driver if he wasn't afraid of the passengers complaining, and the driver said that they were in their own world, and he was bored. He would never guess, dangled the driver, what they had come here for. Finally intrigued, the boy stepped up into the coach.

It's not my first dance with them – I can tell you that they'll swear by it. Great metallic objects in the sky. This is the country for it. The driver stated, generously.

Have you seen them yourself?

I'm a ghost sort of person, the driver said. Now there's something to talk about.

But why here?

The driver nodded up to the mirror, see the tall one with the cap. Back in the day, he and some of the other men were in the air force. They flew out of the big base down that way, and headed over the river, dropping bombs over the hill trails. That's when they started seeing stuff. After the war ended, the tall one came back to see how things looked on the ground. He kept running into people from the bombing group, all looking for the same things, eventually they got together and made a club out of it.

The boy took a seat at the back, to catch the show. The passengers were mainly foreign, they beamed at him, and a girl pressed a cold bottle of water into his hand. It was lively, the guide gripped a microphone, rambling away in a language the boy did not understand. Every once in a while, people would clap, or call out a word, and the guide would look pleased. The way cut across the badlands to a cluster of pedestal rocks. The bus bumped and crawled on the neglected highway, and shadows grew long.

Here, on solid ground, the boy had a clear view of the mushroom rocks. At the centre of this formation was a stocky mesa, a flat mound pushed up from the red earth, redder for the setting sun to the boy's back.

The pilgrims were ecstatic. They hugged each other like pill-heads, and cheered. But as it grew dark, they drew up chairs and sat in silence before the petrified mushroom and their rocky altar. The cold-water woman gave the boy a hotdog and a beer.

The moon rose behind the mountain, and with an eclipse was turned to umbra just as fast. The light extinguished, the devotees began to trot around the site. The boy was loath to join but insistent arms, and smiles won. He circum-ambulated. Steps vanishing in the super fine dust.

When the ritual walk ended there were tears. The boy was instructed to don a blindfold, and still powerless against the tall white people and their local helpers, he sat still in a canvas chair and listened. He heard whirring, and sawing, and gurgling and jingling. Light pierced through the cheap eye-mask, and he felt his skin searing, as under the noon sun.

The boy restrained himself from slipping up a hand to move the mask, as the crowd began scream and moan. He pictured creatures descending with pointed tails, and horned heads, scaly, and grinning as they herded the rich white folk into giant vats, forced them to climb thorny bushes in the nude, and dismembered them with pairs of giant scissors. But he kept the blindfold down until the guide released him. People sat in their chairs admiring the stars and sipping drinks.

What was the trick? The boy asked the guide, but the man shook his head and said that the foreigners were hooked, and it was not for them to judge the goings on.

When the sun came up, they organised games. The foreigners sat in the shade of a mushroom rock and had the locals strip down to their underwear, and crawl along the ground like snakes, and rush back to scale the cliffs like lizards. The tall man handed out prizes to the fastest, who were old men like himself. The losers uncoiled barbed wire and clapped as their comrades ducked in and out of tunnels, and at the centre of their naked labyrinth effected a dance, from which they were eventually released, covered in blood, from tiny razor cuts. When a stocky foreigner, who was still eager to teach, asked the boy if he'd like to be a sapper, like the rest of them, he shook his head.

A bicycle was propped behind the tour bus, and the boy, who had been allowed to slouch off, wasted no time in pedalling away.

With the new day. Clouds gathering out of emptiness were forming into vast and weighty structures. They crawled across the sky, floating into one another like new continents; crushing colour and air, as they pushed out of the sea of blue; bestowing anxiety and expectation on the endless dirt below.

The boy rode through a wasteland. Smoke hung in the air over the flat land, an endless vista of burnt stubble. Ashen scraps caught on the boy's arms and hair. For fun, the boy made lightning which brought down a storm.

The rain came on furiously. Fortune granted the boy a wayside inn, a set of puny cabins just off the main road. At the reception, a girl was transfixed by her phone. The boy asked what she was looking at and if he could have a room. When he had paid for the night, she pushed him a key and said that she was thinking of getting a new job.

Here, this one, it's very popular. On the screen a voluptuous woman, wearing a bikini, was pounding a pestle into a mortar. The boy stared at the looping scene. Here's another one, where she cuts up a chinese cabbage, and another where she cleans some dishes. Do you think I could do that? The boy assured her that she would be just as successful if she set her mind to it. But what's the secret?

It's all in the manner, the boy replied.

The ash and dust from the ride had mostly been washed off in the storm. He hung his clothes out to dry on the porch and lay on the bed watching TV. He went outside to look at the bicycle in his underwear, checking that it was well sheltered and dry. It must have been midnight when the girl from the reception knocked at the door. They had sex.

The boy woke up thirsty, light was streaming into the cabin through the open door. He got down off the bed and walked onto the porch where a bowl of water had been placed on the ground. As the boy began to lap up the water he realised that he had turned into a dog.

The boy barked and ran around the wayside resort. He felt good in his dog form.

Finding it closed, he pissed on the reception door, and began to trot along the highway, following scent. A half-eaten stick of meat greeted him, which he devoured with gusto, before going on his way.

At some point later that day, the boy wandered into a temple complex in search of food and water. He had stopped to lap up brackish water a few times already but it had been hot on the road. His tongue was tiring from hanging out of his mouth, and he could feel foam collecting on his jowls.

Having taken a quick tour of the temple, the boy spied a beaten-up bowl of water, and scraps left by the edge of the monks' dwellings.

The boy's head and tongue sunk into the containers for a length of time, he was consumed with the pleasure of this activity until he noticed the sound of growling.

A pack of five or six dogs had gathered and were approaching steadily with teeth bared. The boy whimpered, looking for an exit but he was trapped.

As the largest of the dogs leapt towards him a jet off water gushed out, accompanied with shouts and reprimands, which were steady and measured, and convinced the dogs to leave.

An old monk waved off the last of the temple mutts. Go on, off with you. I'll feed you later. The monk turned to the boy saying: Poor child, what have you done to yourself?

You are not ready for this. Come here stupid boy.

The monk held out some treats, which he produced from inside his robes and stroked the boy's head.

A witch will do this to you. It's rare but it will wear off eventually, and you'll be OK, if you don't get eaten by the real dogs.

The boy followed the monk to his hut and stepped up on the porch, where he lay down. The monk continued talking to him, in a rolling tone, half to the boy and half to himself.

I know these dogs here. I know them all from the village, the old guys and the young guys, and some of them were monks too.

He started to laugh.

They go from dog to human, just good enough to be human but as humans not quite good enough to remain, so they come back as dogs, over and over again. That's a taste of it – so clean up your act.

The boy ignored most of what the monk was saying and curled up and had a nap.

He stayed at the temple until two visitors appeared one day at the monk's quarters. They sat at the monk's feet on the porch. The monk shooed the boy away, who found a spot in the morning sun at the foot of the cabin.

He lay there listening to the monk chanting, and the fawning sounds issuing from the visitors. After a time, the boy heard the monk conclude with a loud, Sathu.

The boy got up and shook the dust off to see if they might have brought him a treat. The monk patted him on the head affectionately.

You'll take him in your car back to the city, he's a good boy, a bit confused, but that's youth.

TOWNS

The monk finds the boy-dog a ride. At the next town, the Boy meets his former lover and becomes human again.

The visitors tittered nervously at the monk's words. The four of them walked to a pickup truck. Here, insisted the monk, have the boy ride in the cabin. He won't be comfortable in the back.

The monk ushered the boy up into the car. Once he had scrambled in, the boy stood on the driver's seat witnessing as the visitors bowed for a last time to the monk.

As they pulled out, the monk gestured for them to lower the window.

Stay out of trouble young one, I have enjoyed having you here, come back one day as a human, and maybe one day help me when I've taken a wrong turn.

The couple in the car laughed, the boy barked.

The couple were not happy to have the boy in their car. He rocked and drooled between the seats as they headed down the uneven road. Catching sight of himself in the mirror he raised a paw and whimpered, causing the woman to flinch.

The boy heard the couple discussing where to let him out, whether it was wrong to give up on their promise to the monk so soon, whether he was indeed a boy trapped in the form of a dog.

When they reached a town, the man turned to the boy and said: Tell us then, are you a person or are you a dog?

The boy barked, which made the woman cringe once again.

If he is a boy then he did something wrong, and if he is a dog he is not a boy, so either way we should let him out. The woman argued.

After a short lecture about morality, the boy was let down on a side street of the town.

He was glad to get away from the couple, their confusion was irritating him. If they had kept him in the car for much longer, he might have been tempted to bite one of them.

As he looked back at the car, he saw the man brushing off the seats, attempting to remove his hair and some dust he had brought up into the cabin of the pickup truck.

The boy turned and trotted off, nose to the ground.

The boy was on a trail. It led him through the alleyways and along the river promenade of the town. He passed the municipal exercise machines and skirted around the edge of a street market, where people dozed in between the rush hours of meal sessions.

He almost lost the scent once or twice and had to double back. The boy was unfazed by the other street dogs. By now he was an old hand, he walked with a spring in his step, ears and tail up. No one messed with him.

The boy was a good dog.

Finally close, the boy bounded over to the resort girl. She was dressed up, made prettier for the town and whatever business she had there that day.

Cuddling him, she laughed. Not going to bite me. It wasn't so bad, was it? She motioned him to follow her behind a parked truck. He did so bashfully, tail lowering, unsure.

Don't worry, she said. I let go of you. But wasn't it fun? She laughed and squatted. He watched as she let out a stream of urine. Come here, she commanded. And the boy did as bidden. He lapped up her sweet piss as she walked away, her skirt and shirt rearranged.

The boy found a place by the river to lie down. When he woke up, he was himself again.

ORCHARDS AND PADDIES

Travelling by train and foot, he arrives in a town in time to celebrate a festival, he dreams, and is taken in by nudist villagers. Like a figure in a Hindu parable, the Boy ends up with the hermit again.

The boy boarded a southbound train at the station of the small town.

The carriage was empty. He sat looking out at the jagged hills in the distance. A road ran parallel to the tracks. The boy sneered at kids racing their scooters alongside. How pathetic they seemed on their granny bikes. He was ashamed of the passion he had once felt for the little vehicle.

Bored, the boy wandered up the carriage, changing seats, hanging around by the open door. A couple of hours later, at the next stop, he stepped off.

Beyond the station – which was painted jaunty colours, and featured ornate eaves, and pretty shutters, and must have been erected for a passing dignitary – there was nothing remarkable.

The boy imagined the grand figure stepping off the train, a band playing, villagers bowing and averting their eyes. The personage watches the local girls performing a quaint dance, he eats a bite or two and boards the train. No one ever comes again, the table where he ate is carried inside and cordoned off, the station gets a new paint every year, but out and beyond the tracks, nothing.

Green, beyond emerald, incessant green: the paddies, the trees. It made the boy sick to behold this world, all that sweat and care, all the folded-up rice readying itself to be picked, and husked, and traded, and cooked, and eaten, and shat out. He was stuck to the ground, and couldn't move at all, until a woman rode past on a bicycle, with two children clinging to her. Following the mother, he dragged his feet, trying not to look at the fields, and it was with a sigh of relief that he found himself in a sudden shanty, a ribbon of grime, hidden away from the fairytale train station, and the nauseating rice fields.

By a sewer, men were at a game, chucking a coin over a piece of cardboard. They were woodworkers, with sawdust in their hair, and jabbered about the house they had moved that morning. These old wooden houses, all in the wrong place. But did you know, you can cut them off at the legs and hoist them to a better spot. A man with cataracts said, it's a decent living, I'll pass on the secrets, need someone to follow in my steps. But I don't want to spend my days carrying houses, the boy replied, watching a coin flip. The cataract one, now cross, shouted. You're the reason they build of concrete and wire, weak hands, and backs. Losing the argument, the boy was winning the game, banknotes piling up by his marker.

An apprentice, the youngest of the woodmen, showed the boy his gun. He made it when he went to college. It was tube with a nail at one end and carried a single bullet. The young man wet the bullet in his mouth, and the others jeered. The thing blew a bottle off a wall and cast shards of glass over the play area.

Only then did the boy realise, and gently gave back the money, asking to keep a few notes to buy something to eat. As they emptied his pockets, they told him he could keep enough, he really must stick around and see what else they had made. It was over in the field, and he would love it. But the boy bowed out, and they let him go.

With no choice but to brave the rice, the boy marched through paddies, delirious. He spoke to a herd of buffaloes, each with a single white bird on its back, and wasn't sure whether the bird or the buffaloes replied. And the message was repeated by the scarecrows, who flapped. Keep going, on and through the dizzying green, over a hill to a valley.

It was late in the day when the boy arrived in a town. He wanted company but not a soul was about. Despondent, he sat on the curb, and was in danger of reflecting on his predicament when the ground began to shake.

A procession of elderly townsfolk rounded the corner, followed by a converted tour bus. The vehicle had been decked out with lights and speakers and was blasting out a raw sound, bass notes rattling the boy's marrow, and the windows of the deserted shops. Behind this juggernaut came dancers.

The revelry was the town itself. Not a soul apart. In a flash of realisation, the boy perceived the intent which had led him to this spot. He understood for a passing moment his trepidation, in crossing the verdant backways of this county. It had always been arranged that his patron spirit, long lost companion, and favourite ear ghost, who had bequeathed his unnamed gift – that animus, the very same – had brought the boy to acknowledge that this population, celebrating with the onset of night, were his own children, the race born of his wife, and that the boy was here to honour the spirit's most abundant future.

Old ladies performing bird motions cooed at the boy, young lads with staffs and demonic masks shook their fists and hips at girls with flowers in their hair who tittered. The boy was dragged into the crowd and passed a clay-pot, which he swigged, ingesting a liquor which turned through his body.

The night was a circuit, three times round town, the dark hills watching in bemusement. The circle was slow and joined up with those of the years before. The smiles on the boy's face began to ache, as they did on all the initiates. He remembered weeping, along with the others. He remembered being taken in by a family, they had a blanket for him and space on their porch, and he was put to bed under a portable net that looked like a fly cover for a dish of food.

The boy dreamed.

The girl and the boy had been living in the house of a great lord. They spent their days in his compound, looking out at the broad muddy river. The grounds were enclosed by a high wall, and were filled with tall trees, which were full of beautiful birds. They belonged to the lord, who had the wisdom to educate his slaves. It was his eccentricity, he had no children of his own, and only three wives. The lord's passion was for learning. Whenever foreigners came to the city, for trade, he would converse with them and ask if he could perhaps copy any books they had. The girl and the boy were intelligent and soon became his scribes. As his eyesight failed him, the lord had the children recite to him from these tomes.

It came to pass that the king was looking for candidates to oversee a grand construction. The courtiers were not sure if it would be an honour or a punishment and conspired to have the lord selected.

One morning a barge appeared at the lord's private pier. Soldiers stood by as a functionary pronounced. His Majesty the King had decided in his magnanimity to appoint said servant of the crown to the office of royal engineer with the rank of second-class general. The myopic gentleman and members of his household were rushed onto several small craft and after a long and hot day of travel found themselves on the bank of a tributary river at the edge of the jungle, with a simple raised hovel for shelter. They cried that first night, and huddled about each other in fear of the tigers, snakes and forest spirits.

The lord died a few weeks later. He was already old and frail, and the unexpected commission broke his heart. By this time, the small patch of land by the river had been cleared properly, and he had managed to oversee the erection of several dwellings to protect his household. Before he passed away, the lord called the girl and the boy to his bedside.

"You two are my greatest joy and creation. I will depart from this incarnation soon, so I am entrusting the work to you. I have taught you everything I know, you can read our script, that of the Persians, and the Chinese, and a little of the Franks, I leave you my notebooks." He patted two small leather-bound books, made in the Frankish manner. "Inside you will find most of what you need, and many things gleaned from my old library."

The girl and the boy wept. They built him a pyre and chanted with the holy-man who came out of the forest, and disappeared back into it just as mysteriously. They knew that if they were successful the king would let them return to the city, and if they failed in their charge the men would be executed and the women would be sent to the house of pleasure. This was the way it was.

Periodically, according to the rules set down by the moon, the functionary would appear to observe their progress, he would arrange for materials to be sent, half of which would arrive.

What started to take shape, cut from the forest and the soft riverbank was a large and wonderful pleasure garden. At first the girl and the boy worked from designs bequeathed by their deceased patron, but these offered merely the rudiments, a framework. They knew that their garden would need to evoke emotion, reverie, contentment, joy.

Four years previously, in the year of the iron horse, a Greek sailor had arrived in the city, he was called Faulkon. A brilliant trader, engineer and politician, Faulkon soon became the king's most valued advisor. But the king worried that his Faulkon was too far from home, he might one day desire to return to his own lands, the childhood ways, his foreign orchards. Faulkon was a free man, and a Frank, the king knew that even with his great powers, he could not compel the foreigner to stay. And Faulkon was a strange being, by Faulkon's own admission he needed just two wives, stranger still – thought the king – one of these two ladies was a ship.

The king believed that if he could create a labyrinth for this Greek, the man would lose himself in there. A labyrinth, a garden, a forest, a landscape, a world.

A day before the full moon that functionary arrived at the camp. He saw that progress was slow, so he had three of the workers flogged. As he readied himself to leave, he told the girl and the boy, who grovelled by his feet, that they had little time left, if things were not in order, they would both be chained to a corpse for a few nights in punishment.

The girl and the boy worked as best as they could, with their gang of prisoners, and the scant materials to hand.

When the Greek's gilded barge turned the bend of the river, their hearts sank. Faulkon had his own informants, and he was curious what kind of gift he would receive, so that he could measure his response to the king's pleasure.

Faulkon jumped from his vessel, ahead of his attendants, and took a stroll about the work site, while the girl and the boy followed at a respectful distance, ready to explain and ingratiate.

The site had grown immensely, but it was muddy, and unfinished. The Greek asked them what they were up to, and the boy replied that they were building him a garden in the Greek style, a place for him to feel at home, and to rest his lordly soul when he was at leisure. Faulkon looked about at the humid plot and then began to laugh. He slapped the boy on the shoulder and said something incomprehensible in his own tongue.

The girl and the boy watched the unlikely barge leave with tears in their eyes.

That night they made love. They must have been in their twenties by now, five years of captivity after the war had brought them to a place they had been told never to indulge. Your bodies are not yours, your labours are not yours, your next life will still belong to us, what you have is in the past, those evil deeds that saw you taken, that see you here now a slave.

A night bird called plaintively while they fucked for the first time on a pavilion beside the barai, its water covered in lotus flowers.

They resumed their work with a different kind of passion. The garden was not about survival; they were doomed anyway by the cynical Greek and his laughter; the garden was about love.

But what did he see? Why had he not appreciated the works that they had done?

The girl looked back through the lord's notebooks. "These places that we have here, are from Persia, and India, the Khmers, China." She held up the sketches and pointed to the lines of script, the squiggles and characters. "The Frank must have his Greek garden. This is not it."

The boy asked what it was that was Greek, how could they know?

Not caring anymore, they set to work. They gathered some of the workers and made strong ropes from creepers and used them to trap semi-wild elephants. One of the elderly servants remembered how to work the elephants; they now built, hewed, planted in earnest, using all the materials at hand, they plundered the forest for marvellous trees, a jungle tree spewed bees and honeyed blossom, they captured animals that belong in dreams. The park rose up small mountains, lakes, and waterfalls; a monument to their own passions, the things that they would like to see again, the things that they felt inside.

On the day of the inauguration, they waited by the pier but no boat came. The functionary did not arrive that week or the next. Word was to come with the holy-man, who walked out of the forest to tell them that the king had grown tired of the Greek. Faulkon had been executed, and his wife was now a slave in the royal kitchens.

That evening the girl and the boy, woman and man, walked through their creation. They felt something like nostalgia, if they had known the word, they were sad not to show their creations to the Greek.

As the moon came out, they thought they saw a figure wandering in the rose-apple orchard, singing and laughing to himself.

In the early hours the spirit came to him. It needed company, worrying for the souls of its children. Climbing out of the net, the boy went as he would to a startled bird. He followed the spirit out into the banana grove where it lingered between the trees.

His bare feet followed through the orchards and across a stream. The boy walked into the early morning, arriving at a large wooden house on the brink of collapse.

By the now the sun was overhead, and the shadows beneath the raised house were at their deepest.

As the boy stood looking at the house, sure that the sprite had entered the building, and determined somehow to approach and offer comfort, he heard rustling. Two human forms emerged from the bushes behind him. He gaped and stared.

Making their way towards him was an old man carrying a pole with a saw attached to its end, for cutting fruit from a high tree, and an elderly lady bearing a basket full of produce. They were completely naked, and did nothing to hide their bodies, their faces registered no shame. After a moment the boy lowered his eyes.

The old couple gestured to his feet, which were muddy. The naked old man pointed him over to a hose.

They sat under the eaves of the old house eating sticky-rice. The boy soon learned how to ignore their silence and their nudity. The wrinkled skin did not disturb him. The room they led him to was clean and pleasant. It had a bed and a mosquito net, and he was thankful for it.

The old couple were not the sole inhabitants, their household consisted of a son and daughter-in-law, and several other people who lived in outer buildings and may have been their former servants – back when they all used to wear clothes.

During the day they worked the fields and orchards. They used no electricity and insisted on the strictures of dumb autarky.

The boy did not know how long it had been since they spoke. Their sign language was easy to understand, within a month the boy was able to communicate, by the end of the rainy season his clothes were threadbare and he was fluent in their silent tongue.

The daughter-in-law was chatty, a gossip, who was restless and once liked to sing. She signed their tale one day as the boy helped fix an old lock-dam in the woods. Apart from some bartering, they were no-longer in touch with the locals, who lived some kilometres away, as the boy knew. He might not have noticed some of the peculiar practices that were going on in the district. It was an unseemly thing to speak of and she didn't want to have to dwell on it but it all began for very urgent and practical reasons. There had been a spate of unexplained deaths in the community. He might have seen it in the news a few years ago, all these young men dying so tragically in their sleep. At the time, she was particularly afraid since she had just got married, her husband had lost three of his friends in the past months. She prayed constantly, fearing that he would be next.

One day a man appeared at the edge of the main village. He sat down by the road and began to enact a ritual, and said that if they were to listen the tragedies might cease. The villagers began to hang shirts outside of their homes, understanding that a violent spirit had come, and could only be appeased by this sign of humility.

The chatterbox was going to continue when they were interrupted by the appearance of her husband who looked angry. She dropped her hands immediately.

The boy was fine living with this family. The farm was very peaceful, and he liked his room. He got on well with most of the small community, and enjoyed the quiet, which had crept up on him, as if all the noise of his past years was finally falling from him. But ultimately it was not a place of tranquillity, and if it was placid there, it came with a price.

The tacit choice presented to the boy was between nudity and the road. Within a few days he was travelling again, the weather had an edge to it, the underlying chill of the changing season. His threadbare clothes did little against the morning cold, but he felt exhilarated.

At a village, he stepped through a door into a slum, crowded with faces, and pungent with effluence. The eyes of the community were away from him, and from there he trod through a large and equally distracted city, at the end of which was a paddy, and a canal and an orchard of pomelo trees.

Standing in the woods, he noticed the calluses on his hands. If he could see his face, the boy wondered, would he find he was old already?

Hearing a voice the boy turned.

What is time after all but an illusion? If I were to hold up a mirror, would you choose to see the child of yesterday or the weathered man of today, or the corpse of tomorrow?

The boy stared at the hermit realising that he had been everywhere and nowhere.

The boy was still listening to the hermit's story, in the highlands by the communist camp, which could go on for another kalpa – as the seas emptied out in noodle spoon measures and the mountains wore down with the brushing of a feather.

Bowing his head in respect to the hermit, the boy inquired if there was perhaps a short cut he could take. The reply was gnomic, and saw the boy walking into the depths of a cave.

RIVER LIFE

Drinking and fighting, the Boy floats along a river. Multitudes of wild animals, escapees from a private zoo, line the riverbanks, the Boy listens to a story about a tiger spirit.

The boy dangled his feet off the side of a rice barge. He gazed at the slow rolling riverbanks.

The boat family was cooking, frying chillies that made him sneeze. They laughed and called out: Almost ready, come and eat. They spread out a mat on the deck and gathered round, squatting to reach into the bowls, a couple of women, men, some children. They spoke quickly, half in dialect but the boy could catch most of what they said.

When he looked up from the meal, the riverbanks had gone, a great flood had swallowed up the land, punctuating the water, stick-like, was a petrol station logo and a tip of a pylon.

That sunset was almost too brilliant for the boy, the red had nowhere to go in this endless mirror, and he thought he was on fire over the water. Afterwards he slept uneasily, over the leaden flood and the juddering engine.

It might have been despair, at the plight of the land, or just the devilish effect of too much light, but the men began to drink, they challenged the boy to a shot or two which he declined. Had not the hermit told him to be wary of his tongue and try to avoid liquor? They mocked him and shoved a bottle at his face, and before long the boy found himself pushing and yelling like the rest of them, animated by the same desire to feel – to be hurt. As one, the men and women, began to hit each other, seeking victory in oblivion. Shortly the boy, another winner, was unconscious on the deck.

He woke up on a sheltered pier with a sore head and a sticky mouth. The water had subsided, and he took a moment to admire the beautiful teak bench where he had slept, that was polished from use. It made him feel such a great sense of unity with all the others who had been at this place, that there was no need to name it. As he was philosophising in his way, the boat family came back bearing noodles and soup in plastic bags. Like the boy, their eyes were blackened from the fighting, but they too smiled with tenderness.

From the river, they watched a pair of panthers take down a large sambar deer. They saw lions, and elephants, and confused zebras – escapees from a private park, set free by the flood. The boy and his bruised companions admired these creatures, and with the night shared a dream of luxuriant hybridisation, of the new species that would come about, as order broke down: new configurations made flesh.

The river was wide, and the boy hoped that it would carry them all the way to the coast, and out beyond the famous sandbank, into the gulf, to the open sea, and, with that promise, onwards and onwards. But the way was clogged with hyacinth, and debris. A collapsed bridge forbade them passage.

They turned, shivering at the fate they avoided – the toxic carpet out there can reach up and pull you overboard, can't you hear the calls of those who drowned? Heading back upstream, the craft wheezed against the current, and soon a narrow tributary was spotted where they branched off.

The canal was calm, almost stagnant, its waters were dark and pungent. They followed it until the barge reached an impasse and could continue no further, finding a landing flanked by stone lions. They cut the engine and tethered the boat, unsure of disembarking – and argued not to do so unless they were alone. What if the sunken bridge had been a trap?

The jetty was covered in drying leaves and mulch. The boy jumped down, exhorting the others. Nature has taken back what is hers. Come. He ran along a walkway, feet soft on the muck, beside a sculpted balustrade. Stairs rose to a lawn ringed by topiary animals, behind which was a large white house, bigger than any the boy had seen. In his excitement, the boy was separated from his companions, and only glanced back when he was halfway across the lawn, noticing their fear-smiles, and then the apology of abandonment.

Without turning, the boy knew that the big house had sent its people to take him, flight was futile. He was the offering, and the boat crew were free after rendering a body as gift. He was as quiet as his captors, but not as calm.

Thronged, the boy was taken across a wide terrace, passing a disused swimming pool, to an entrance to the house. The boy felt sorry and hopeless, and tried to concentrate on the good things in life, but all that he could muster was the image of the pearl-green bike, that had got him into so much trouble.

A seance was in progress. At the far end, beneath the vaults of the grand room, with its landscapes and heritage painting, presided a figure. People sat cross-legged or with their legs drawn behind, politely. Their decorum was fitting, and as kitsch as the house, a relic of the 90s. The devotees shuffled aside as the boy was led to the front, where a lady was seated in a large, gilded chair. Not knowing what to do, the boy prostrated himself, which raised a murmur of approval. Things were going well, the boy told himself from the ground, all he needed to do was keep grovelling.

She was heavily made up, it was hard to say her age, neither too young, nor too old. Her clothes looked expensive, she had on high heels, and rings, beads of pearls, and layers of glinting necklaces, as if she had raided a gold shop. An attendant, sitting at her feet, was holding a handbag, to the other side, another gripped a receptacle, into which the lady flicked ash from her cheroot.

The boy sat holding his hands together in supplication. Waiting to be spoken to. The lady puffed and glanced around the room, until her supporters had settled down.

You, she nodded to the boy, come here. She touched his head. Are you afraid? What should we do with you? Before he could answer, she began to intone, her face taking on a severity, as if she was drawing down something with the words – sounds which made the boy's heart beat faster. The chant was unsettling, not the calming prayers or even the undulating mantras he had heard from monks, these were guttural, primal sounds. The boy felt his insides turning, the fluttering of a soul seeking escape. The lady stopped suddenly, then, having looked inside the boy, fixed him with a contemptuous glare. You want to know but you block your ears, she said with a raspy voice.

I can't do much with you. Tell me child, why did you come here?

Your people brought me here.

She shook her head. They did no such thing. He was about to object when she waved a hand at him. We are none of us free. It is all worked out. They were here to receive you.

Yes, I came here to see you, he obliged.

You came here to ask me something? He thought of something but held his tongue. He was sure she could read his mind. She blew smoke his way, and the question popped into his head, it was not his own. Where did we come from and where are we going?

This one brought a smile to the lady's face. The crowd was pleased too, a scribe began to write as she began.

A long time ago, in a village beside a great river, there lived a young couple. The wife would weave, cook, and help sow the rice. The husband fished, foraged, watched the animals, and enjoyed hunting. Like all the others in the village, the couple were content. With three harvests each year, there was never a shortage of food. Nature provided the materials for clothing, shelter, and boats; it protected and nurtured the community. Neighbouring communities were spread up and down the river, and with such distance between them, disputes seldom arose.

At the heart of the settlement was a small temple, erected in times beyond memory by the ancestors of people who had once been in these parts. The villagers were proud of their temple, but they understood that to remain in good fortune, they must also propitiate the wild forces that prowled in the forest, the spirits of place, and the dangerous animals that roamed at night. They knew fear, even though life was so peaceful, and held in awe the spirits of tigers that lived in the forest.

"Never look at a tiger spirit," children were warned. "If the tiger ghost should come, you must look away, for it might show mercy; dare to peek, and it will never let you go. If one should come close, empty your mind and stay still – do as the trees in the wind, it will blow away. Remain as dull as the riverbed stones, let the angry spirit wash over and away."

"Nothing bad will happen," the wise taught, "as long as we remain dutiful, offer rice and our innocence."

One day, it was the couple's turn to visit the forest shrine. This came at an auspicious moment, since she had begun to feel a change in her body. Alert and cautious, the pair made their way into the woods along a well-worn track and soon reached the foot of an old tree, its crown towering above the canopy. Beside this giant was a strange stone, jutting out of the ground like a big tooth. It had been tied with coloured threads and greying cloth, while nearby in the clearing stood a small wooden altar, perched on a single leg and covered in drying garlands from the last visitors.

Arriving, the couple began to clear the hallowed space, removing fallen branches and cutting back the creeping foliage. Absorbed in their task, not a word was said. It was better to stay quiet and not think. And yet, even though she had been there many times before, the woman's mind strayed to the baby growing inside her. Meanwhile, her husband slipped into a circular reverie about a recent hunt, fresh blood on his hand, and a mild rivalry with one of his companions. Both tried to clear these thoughts, but the distractions kept returning.

Without guile, they had erred. Although the sacrilege was mere complacency, it was upon them. The woman noticed it first: an unnatural shade had fallen over her hand, the way her husband's foot tripped where it should not have, a hush followed by the rustling that was now coming from the forest. She gazed at her partner, who was brushing the altar with a distant look in his eyes. She touched him, and beckoned. The woman and the man, young and careless, had called into the woods, and the woods had answered. Painfully aware of their predicament, the couple sat praying to be forgiven.

The sound of leaves crunching underfoot was accompanied by the smell of rotting meat. The creature approached brazenly, impossible to ignore or dream away. It was forbidden to look. As children, they had played the tiger game to see who could keep their eyes shut longer, but as adults, the couple failed, too scared and too curious – perhaps fated – because their eyes opened without volition at the same time.

A beast, large and majestic, shimmering out of the jungle and looking so much like a real tiger, was standing a few metres away. If it had been a tiger, flight would have been futile. The predator would have slaughtered the weak humans before they got to their feet. This was not a tiger; their prospects were worse. Fragile and tender, the woman and the man reached out and touched hands, their breath coming in gasps, their hearts pounding. It's one thing to preach stillness and emptiness of body and mind, but in the presence of the spirit, self-control was impossible.

The tiger-ghost moved slowly. A hot, fetid air enveloped them, the stench of death. The man knew this scent; it was the chase, the breath and sweat of hunters jabbing with spears and pulling at ropes. It was the animal giving up its life in cries and panic. The man felt the tiger's whiskers touch his shoulder, burning his skin. The woman knew the odour too; it was also of sex and birth. She had helped to deliver and recognized the smell of the nether regions, of the bowels and blood, that bring life.

The ghost-tiger circled, then came to a stop and spoke: "Do not think that I have been called. I have always been close, wherever it is dark, wherever you have feared to tread, I was there. Do not fear for your lives; I have come to make a simple proposition." The voice was velvety, rich, and resonant – more than human. They were being addressed by a god.

The woman felt a pain in her womb. "It will be ours," the voice said, and she shuddered, then nodded. In her terrifying discomfort, she sensed the tiger leap towards her husband, all she could make out were murmurs. What passed between them would remain a secret. The words that came into the man's ear from the tiger were new, and lingered, turning into a grammar, allowing ideas that were exciting and shameful.

Abruptly, like the passing of a storm, the tiger was gone. The couple sat petrified for some time afterwards. Coming round, they bowed their heads to the tree, stone, and altar, feeling weak yet giddy. Then they noticed something foreign lying on the ground. The man reached across and picked up the object. It was a stone nugget, an amulet. The charm was jet-black and polished, shining even in the half-light of the forest clearing. It was flat; one side seemed to have been carved, the other was smooth. It was cool to the touch and unlike anything either of them had ever set eyes on.

Unsure of what to do and still shaken up, they pondered leaving the amulet on the altar, reasoning it was not clear what this thing meant or what it could bring. If the other villagers found out, discord would arise. Nothing must be said of the encounter, for they would be ostracized from the village as impure. Being touched by something divine could only bring fear.

The man dug a hole between the tree's roots and was about to bury the talisman when he paused. Tearing the silk bag they had used to carry the offerings, he fashioned a belt, into which he twisted the stone, and slipped his knife.

Drawing close to the village, they smelled smoke and heard screams. From a vantage point, the couple saw an attack – men coming by river in three paddle boats, to plunder and enslave. The woman turned to her partner and said it was good for him to hunt, for the sake of the unborn child. The man cast off his doubts and climbed down the forested slope to the river. He swam to the boats, killing the guards, and went from there into the settlement and out of sight. She watched as the attackers fled, with only enough of them left to fill a single boat.

The villagers were saved, and although they knew that something was lost, there was nothing to be said. For by a miracle and a great act of bravery, most had their lives and freedom. It was whispered that in the midst of the tragedy, the man came to them, but he was not himself and had revelled in the carnage.

In the coming days, not satisfied with seeing off the war-party, the man led his own people downstream, returning with trophies and captives who were pledged to follow and serve him. The river and the large forest that had never known anything but peace and simple prosperity had now been awakened. It had been forged by violence into an entity with a hunger.

Soon the couple and their young boy were living in a large compound, with loyal people waiting on them. Raised up, they could see their future: the amulet passing to the child, who would be known by name, the founding of their line, the generations ahead. It would be said that the family were like tigers among men, always voracious, no longer just avenging or defending but expanding, looking for new places and new people to capture and lead. Always at the head of this would be the black stone, and somewhere lost in time a children's story.

The man and the beautiful woman had understood the curse. Although they never spoke of it, both thought often of that day in the forest and what had been promised and lost. They imagined casting the stone into the river or properly burying it by the ancient tree. But the couple knew that the stone was just a symbol; what had become could not be undone so easily. The rapacious force brought into their lives was ever watchful and judging. It could never be compelled and was in constant need of conquest. However, the hunger, which was its essence, grew with each exploit, pushing it through the realms of men and gods. Not sated with the present, it would devour the past, and all that had pertained to here – every shade and nuance of former action – would be consumed, and by this logic, it would come upon itself.

Sometimes as the lady spoke, her eyes were closed, and she rolled along through the tale but at the end she just looked straight in the boy's eyes, into and through him.

Do you see now, why we are where we are?

No, I don't.

You don't want to?

I don't want to see.

Better, the lady said, giving her handbag a furtive look, before taking up her cheroot, and dismissing the boy.

The boy was alone again, he walked, knowing that his feet were better than his head.

THE CITY AND THE SUBURB

The Boy has grown old. Soldiers drive him to the city, as he makes his way through the troubled metropolis an amulet talks to him. The Boy creeps back into the forgotten suburb from whence he came, carrying a special gift from his spirit friend.

Passive and pensive, the boy was in the shade of a large rain tree when a truck pulled up beside him.

The soldiers told him they had instructions to give him a ride. The boy found himself sitting with a group of young men who addressed him as elder, the boy didn't know why.

The soldiers grew quieter and more nervous as they began to approach the city, with its sprawling nowhere of warehouses, and traffic. The man who let him down from the back of their truck had a sweaty palm. An officer flagged down a car and talked to the driver. A few minutes later the boy was sitting in the back seat of a vehicle.

He recognised them for having given him a lift when he was a dog. Somehow the monk and the officer and the car seemed to thread together. The couple of course did not recognise him, but once again were unhappy at having to give the boy a ride.

Where are you going? The man dispassionate, the car redolent with jasmine and spring-onion.

Home.

Where is that?

By the sea.

Which part of the coast, east or west?

By the river and to the west, where the dead come from – where I came from and where I am returning to. The driver shrugged as if he knew, although in the mirror, the boy could see that he was lost – so the boy took a moment to admit that he had once been a dog, and they had thrown him out, but he was not upset, because in the end, they had reached the same place, and there was something to be said about that.

Neither the woman nor the man looked back, and this was normal, since their eyes were for the destruction being wrought on the city as they drove. The man nodded, he may have a said a word or two, but it was obvious to the boy that there was really no use in conversing with them.

He would perhaps have rested had not the talisman on the dashboard of the car begun to talk. The boy was not alarmed, and listened as the rocky fellow explained that he been picked up for a greasy note from a sidewalk vendor.

They didn't know what a treasure they had acquired. The charm could bring love – see how the driver and his wife glow – and keep you from drunkenness – which is to say, you could go out and have a good time. They bought me, the amulet blathered, with their last savings, thinking I would turn their fortunes around. Gold and safety, that's what they requested. I'm quite the opposite.

These are days of semblance. They only got me because you're supposed to have something watching over the car – anything will do, that's what these folk imagine. People these days are full of ideas, thin on action, weak on knowledge. If you ask me, it's all understandable, too much change, no idea of what is what. It's little wonder that people do things without knowing why or to what end. But I'll give you some advice, the dashboard sprite went on, you'll do well to get another ride, these two are terminal.

In a few weeks the sober man will find out she's having an affair, and get shot by the lover. A day or two later the lovers will drive me around town and get into an accident – I'm really not for road safety – and I'll go back to the earth.

The boy listened until he could take no more, then jutted his chin and pushed forward between the front seats to say: Disgraceful incarnate, enough with the confusion – what role have you played in this calamity, isn't there anything you could have done? Look at this two, so in debt they barely own the clothes on their backs, will be paying off this car for the next lifetime, it's no surprise they turn to false idols like you for help.

The couple gaped at the boy, with his one-sided row, and let him out as soon as they could, while he pointed fingers at the grinning talisman, and tried, vainly, to warn the pair, who turned their heads from him and pretended it hadn't happened until the car door was closed, upon which they drove steadily away, without looking in the rear view mirror, for even a second, to see if the crazed passenger was still shouting.

The boy climbed over a barricade. He could hear gunfire and smell smoke. He stepped over the sandbags and began to make his way through the scarred buildings. After a time, he was back by the river, and the sounds of the battle were subsiding.

For hours, the boy didn't see a soul. It was not hot, he walked leisurely. When he spied someone up ahead, trudging along the same empty road, he called out, but the figure didn't stop or turn, and kept going always at the same distance.

By the time the boy had reached the places that he knew, the spectre had vanished, and he wondered if it had been trying to lead him, trick, or quicken him. He walked faster now. Almost home. Inevitably, the boy thought about his childhood and early memories by the river, near the warm sea.

The tide was in as he passed. He saw the spire of a temple rising out of the waves, he saw the remains of villages along the coastline. There is nothing left but to go home, he said to himself, the sea is in, and I'm no wiser.

Three coins jingled in his pocket. Feeling them, he thought of the hermit who had given them to him and of the road as he had known it.

Nearing his alleyway, the boy stepped past greying dog shit, and threw the coins over his shoulder – to dissuade any spirits that he had encountered from following. Before going home, the boy decided to stop at his girlfriend's house.

In their places: the evening neon lights of the cruciform estate, the brittle house, the mango tree darkening luxuriantly, his girl's dad washing the car, a t-shirt drawn up over a potbelly. The boy stopped to say hello and hear that he had lost weight. They spoke for a few minutes about nothing much before the boy went inside. The girl was scrolling through images on her phone. She looked pleased to see him. Did you come from far? Just down the road, he replied, and felt tired by his inability to make any sense of life.

After such a long journey, the boy thought he should have gone home first. But by now the family had gathered to see him. To the expectant faces of his girlfriend, her grandmother, younger brother, a nephew, sister-in-law, mum and dad, the boy announced that he had something to show them. With nothing from his travels but the spirit's gift, he asked them to turn off the lights. Opening his hand, the boy revealed a flame sitting in his palm. It flickered and beckoned and didn't burn, and in unison they said a word of approbation, and were glad to have the boy back. It wasn't much, it was enough, the boy was happy.

Born in Cambridge, and raised in Greece, Shane Bunnag is Thai and British. He studied history and has worked as a filmmaker, photographer and writer. *The Twenty-Five Fifties* is his first novel, it draws from a time of traversing Thailand while making a series of documentaries: *Walking Klongtoey*, *During the Flood*, *Elephant Shaman*, and *Marnram*. He is the author of *Chariot of the Sun*, and *Barbary Figs*, a photography book.

www.shanebunnag.com